THREE TALES

R. E. WRIGHT

Published 2025

Printed in the United States of America

First Edition
ISBN (softcover): 978-1-963380-95-8
ISBN (e-book): 978-1-963380-96-5

For information, address:
Holzer Books LLC
8 The Green, Ste. A
Dover, Delaware 19901 USA

For information about special discounts available for bulk purchases, sales promotions, and educational needs, contact:
info@holzerbooksllc.com
+1 (888) 901-7776

Contents

THE UNSUSPECTING WIDOW

A special thanks to Akira Kurosawa and "Rashomon"

Martha pulled down the ladder from the ceiling in the hallway and climbed into the attic. She had not been up there since her mother died—years ago. Then her father died, and her cousin Ruth died. Joe, her husband, had placed things in the attic after each death. But then Joe died. So many years had passed. The last of her children had left. Now she was alone—completely alone.

She entered the dusty attic, dimly lit by a beam of sunlight streaming through the single window at the front end of the space. Cardboard boxes and wooden crates were everywhere. She had set her mind on finding some old photographs from an earlier time in her life. As she searched through the nearest boxes, she noticed an old trunk with a rounded top tucked beneath the back-corner rafters. Curious, she walked over to it. She couldn't remember ever seeing this trunk before. She pulled the chain for the lone light bulb hanging from the rafters, knelt in front of the trunk, and slowly undid the brass latches before opening it.

Martha first saw three black candles tied together with hemp. A black-and-white photo of an unknown couple in late Victorian dress sat in a frame adorned with shells. She found three locked books that appeared to be diaries. There were three eagle feathers, a hunting knife in a scabbard with traces of blood on the blade and handle, a bunch of dried flowers, a wedding dress, and a pair of men's spats—along with other clothes and objects.

Martha was intrigued by the wedding dress. When she pulled it out, it looked as if it had never been worn. It was her size, so she stripped down to her underclothes and slid into the dress. Pulling it up over her hips and buttoning it all the way to the collar beneath her chin, she wondered who it had belonged to. It was a perfect fit. She went over to the full-length mirror in the attic and saw that the reflection was not her own. The image was completely unlike her in size and distinguishing features—hair, eyes, and every facial and bodily detail. The woman had dark hair and eyes and wore a gray dress much like the one in the photograph. The image mirrored all of Martha's movements and poses, as a looking glass normally does. Then the woman in the mirror began to speak. Martha stepped away and tried to assure herself that she was not dreaming or hallucinating.

When she returned to the mirror, the woman was still speaking. Martha hadn't paid attention to what the woman was saying at first, but now she realized the woman was telling the story of her life.

"My parents were from the Old Country. They immigrated here shortly after the Civil War. Of course, they brought with them their culture and customs. They had..."

The woman had reached the point in her story when she was about twelve years old, and then her image began to dim—until she disappeared.

The woman had captured Martha's interest with her story. Martha knew it wasn't finished—it had broken off mid-sentence—and she wanted to hear the rest. She returned to the trunk and took out the diaries. Breaking the lock on one, she opened it and was shocked to find only blank pages. The second and third diaries yielded the same result. Frustrated, Martha frantically rummaged through the rest of the trunk's contents.

She found more clothes, including a waistcoat, a gray dress with a high collar, and a pair of men's knickerbockers. She also found more photographs, a pair of round-framed spectacles, and a leather-bound Bible. Inside the Bible's cover, she discovered birth certificates and a parchment on which the following couplets were written in ink:

When doth wish to hear me speak,
Find a way to ignite me.

I never appear nakedly;
I'm attired, for heaven's sake.

My actions I've thought to be noble;
Others may not see it so.

I fly on wings till I am no more—
Why and how, when my story is told.

Martha didn't know what to make of the parchment; the lines appeared to be riddles. She desperately wanted to hear the woman in the mirror speak again. Still wearing the wedding dress, she recalled the first lines: "Find a way to ignite me."

She thought of the candles. Lighting one, she crept to the mirror. Nothing happened. She lit a second candle, but it wasn't until she lit the third that the woman in the mirror reappeared. Martha poured hot wax onto the floor in front of the mirror and stood the candle upright. The woman identified herself as Elizabeth Tate and began her story.

"I was the oldest girl in the family, and when I was twelve, in accordance with my parents' tradition, I was betrothed to William P. Degas III. There was no objection on my part; I understood that it was simply the way things were among my people. It was rare for individuals to marry alone—families married families. Besides, William was very handsome. He was well liked in school, had good prospects, and came from a successful family. William and I had many wonderful times. We went everywhere together—horseback riding, ice skating, parties, church teas—everywhere. Both of our parents wanted us to be together as much as possible. After all, we were expected to spend the rest of our lives together, and they thought we should get to know each other before marriage.

When I was fifteen and William was sixteen, his father's business partner, Alexander Monet, and his wife died in a train accident. Fortunately, their only child—a boy named Gerald—was at home with his nanny. There were no close relatives who could take him in, so William II, William's father, volunteered to adopt the Monet boy.

When Gerald, who was the same age as William, joined the Degas household, we became a group of three. He accompanied William and me on our outings and fit in well.

Two years later, William left home for college. Months afterward, Gerald and I became romantically interested in each other. That interest soon turned into love, and I began lying—not only to William and my family about our relationship, but also to myself. The guilt began to torment me, but it didn't stop Gerald and me from meeting in secret.

When William came home for Christmas during his second year at school, I could tell he sensed something had changed in the way Gerald and I interacted. But it wasn't until he returned in the spring of the following year that his suspicions grew strong enough to confront Gerald.

Gerald tried, but he couldn't hide the truth, and the two came to blows. William got the better of him, and after the fight, he headed for my house.

Gerald took a small-caliber handgun that belonged to Mr. Degas and set out in hot pursuit.

I was in my family's garden when William approached me. He was like a raging maniac.

He grabbed me by the arm and began cursing me.

I struggled with him and tried to pull away. I scratched his face and neck.

He pulled a hunting knife and stabbed me in the lower chest and abdomen—just as Gerald found us in the garden.

Gerald tried to stop the assault, but William turned on him and stabbed him in the chest.

Gerald aimed a small revolver at William and shot him in the face. Though bleeding profusely, he rushed to me and cradled me in his arms as I lay on the ground.

He screamed for help, but no one came; my parents were not home.

He collapsed—and both of us died in each other's arms."

Martha was shocked—she had never expected the story to take such a turn. After telling her tale, Elizabeth's image began to dissolve and fade from the mirror. Martha was eager to hear the other stories; after all, there were three characters and three candles. She placed a label with Elizabeth's name on the floor where the candle had stood and extinguished it. Then she began to remove the wedding dress and returned to the trunk to put it away. As she sifted through the trunk again, she noticed the gray dress now had two slits—one in the bust and another in the waist.

Martha took out another candle. She studied the photograph of the couple again. The man in the photo wore a pair of round spectacles and a waistcoat.

She had put her skirt back on, but now she also donned the waistcoat and the eyeglasses. She lit a candle and went to the mirror—nothing. Martha snuffed it out, lit the remaining candle, and returned to the mirror. This time, a young man appeared. He was tall, with dark curly hair. He wore no waistcoat but had those familiar round glasses. He said he was William Degas—and then he began his story.

"I was an only child, which may have led to me being somewhat spoiled. My father and his partner, Alexander Monet, owned a very successful construction business in Charlotte, North Carolina. Alexander had a son, Gerald. We were the same age, and from the time we were both eleven, we became good friends.

When I was thirteen, my parents arranged a future marriage for me to a young girl named Elizabeth, from the family of a friend who came from the same country as we did. She and I became good friends. We went everywhere together. We were more like brother and sister than a betrothed couple. I had no real idea what marriage meant at that age, but as I grew older, I began to understand. The more I got to know Elizabeth, the more my love for her blossomed.

At sixteen, Gerald lost both of his parents in a train accident. My father took him in, and our friendship became very close. Gerald joined

Elizabeth and me in all our activities. The three of us formed a formidable trio in our social circle.

At eighteen, I went away to college, while Gerald opted to stay home and learn more about the construction business. He learned how to read and execute blueprints and took an apprentice position as a site foreman. The portion of the company's profits that would have been his father's was placed in a trust fund for him.

Anyway, when I left for college, Elizabeth's parents and mine planned for us to be married after I finished my second year. I didn't go home in the spring of my first year because college had placed many unexpected demands on me. I didn't return until the summer. By that time, many wedding preparations had already been made, though the ceremony was still a year away. Elizabeth's mother had taken her to be fitted for her wedding dress. She had booked the hall for the reception and contacted the church and the pastor to reserve a date. That first summer was wonderful. Both Elizabeth and Gerald wanted to know everything about college: What was the campus like? What activities was I involved in after classes? What new people had I met?

When I went home for Christmas that first year, I noticed that Elizabeth and Gerald were acting differently—in the way they looked at each other and in the way they spoke. It didn't sit right with me. I tried to ignore my suspicions, but they lingered in the back of my mind.

I went back to school after Christmas break, but I couldn't concentrate on my studies. I began writing to Elizabeth. Those letters were the most sorrowful correspondence I had ever written—it was clear what I wanted to ask, but I avoided coming right out and saying it. I approached my suspicions obliquely. Through a series of letters exchanged between us, I gathered from Elizabeth's words that Gerald was still her friend, just as he had always been—nothing had changed. The little reassurance I drew from our letters helped the time pass more quickly. I intended to go home that spring break.

When I arrived at the house, my parents weren't there. They hadn't expected me, and I hadn't expected them to be gone. I found Gerald in the backyard; he was repairing something or other. I was more direct with him than I had been with Elizabeth. He knew full well that she and I were to be married in a couple of months.

The louse began boasting about their relationship. With no respect for Elizabeth or me, he spoke crudely about "breaking her in" for me—taking her virginity. Then he turned and walked back toward the house.

I followed him and grabbed him by the back of his shirt at the doorway.

That was when the fight began.

We fought from the back porch into the kitchen, and I must admit, Gerald was getting the better of me—until I remembered the small revolver my father kept in a kitchen drawer.

I raced to the drawer and pulled out the gun. I pointed it at Gerald and warned him to back off.

He charged at me. I shot him in the face.

I cannot say it was an accident. Gerald was dead, and I was shaking like a leaf in a strong breeze. I was frozen in time—I didn't know what to do. I dropped the gun and made my way to the Tate household as quickly as I could.

As I approached the house, I saw that Mr. and Mrs. Tate were in the front parlor. I don't know where Elizabeth's siblings were, but I could see her working in the garden out back.

I walked down the side path and approached her. I was still shaking and sweating heavily by that point.

She ran to me with a worried look in her eyes and asked what was wrong. I told her that Gerald and I had fought, but she no longer had to worry about him making any advances toward her. I could barely get the story out—the story that ended with me shooting him in the face.

Elizabeth was weeping. She cried out in a high, shrill voice, "William, how could you! We were lovers! I spoke to my parents—we were going to speak to yours about the wedding when you came home. Oh my God, how could you do this?"

She was holding a hori-hori knife, one edge sharp and the other serrated. She plunged it into my neck. I fell to my knees, and in my last bit of consciousness, I heard Elizabeth say, "This is all my fault."

She committed hara-kiri by stabbing the hori-hori into her midsection, driving it horizontally, and then pulling it straight up the middle."

William's image began to grow dimmer and dimmer—then vanished with a poof.

Martha was troubled and confused by the differences in the stories. She left William's candle standing on the floor, a short distance from Elizabeth's, and labeled the spot in front of it with his name.

Martha returned to the trunk. The only remaining men's clothing items were a pair of knickerbockers and a pair of spats. As funny as they looked worn together, Martha donned them. She went to the mirror, and Gerald Monet's image appeared. He was of average build, with dark hair and blue eyes, dressed smartly in 1890s attire—a long cutaway coat and a top hat. Martha sat in a chair in front of the mirror, and just like that, Gerald mirrored her movements and sat in a chair facing her. She lit the third candle and Gerald Monet's image appeared.

He talked about losing his parents—about how grief-stricken and insecure he felt. When he was taken in by the Tates, he began to feel more secure, but he always believed he wasn't getting a fair shake in his father's business dealings. He was young and didn't know enough about the business to truly assess the company's viability, but that was simply what he believed.

"William and I became good buddies—partners in crime. We came from well-to-do families at the time. We ran in tandem as we competed for the girls. We had plenty of friends. We had plenty of parties.

I knew that William was to marry Elizabeth—this had been arranged when they were children. But I never expected William to follow through with the marriage. He and I had always believed the times were changing, and that the custom of being paired as bride and groom by our parents was antiquated. Besides, Elizabeth was one of us. She was a third of our group.

About six months after William left for college, however, Elizabeth and I grew closer—close enough to make me believe she didn't truly believe in the marriage planned since childhood. It was the way our casual, accidental touches sparked emotion; the way we looked at each other and hung on every word the other spoke. Soon, we began to talk about our feelings and share our secrets.

I had fallen in love with Elizabeth, and I believed she had fallen in love with me. Between the time William left for college in September of 1892 and returned for Christmas that same year, our relationship had progressed from a single kiss to the ultimate act of intimacy.

That Christmas, William seemed very distant toward both Elizabeth and me. He wasn't as engaging or open as he had been in the past. Maybe he was facing some hard choices at school. Perhaps he had sensed that something had changed between Elizabeth and me, though we tried not to show it. William went back to school after the New Year. I never spoke to Elizabeth about it, and she never brought it up.

No one was expecting William to come home for spring break during his second year. Mr. and Mrs. Degas had taken their daughter and youngest son to Durham to visit Mrs. Degas's aunt, who had been sick for several weeks.

I was left home alone. Neither Elizabeth nor I heard William when he walked through the door. However, we did hear him call out my name before knocking on my bedroom door, opening it, and discovering Elizabeth and me in a compromising situation.

William lunged at me from the doorway and grabbed me by the throat.

We fought from the bed to every corner of the bedroom. William was actually getting the better of me.

But then I grabbed the hunting knife from my dresser and managed to cut him twice before he ran from the room.

Elizabeth was hysterical, weeping uncontrollably. I was sitting on the bed, holding her and trying to console her, when William came back into the room with a revolver.

He aimed it at me, but before he could pull the trigger, Elizabeth threw herself over me, and he shot her twice in the back.

I rushed him before he could fire again and plunged the knife into his chest.

But my body was pressed up against the barrel of his gun, and William fired again."

The mirror went black.

Martha was startled by the suddenness of it. She let out a heavy sigh and rose from the chair, feeling drained, exhausted, and very confused. She snuffed out the last candle, which she had placed in relation to the other two to form a perfect triangle.

She returned to the trunk and placed the spats and knickerbockers back inside. Then she picked up one of the diaries and found William's complete story written on its pages, just as he had presented it to her. The same was true for Elizabeth and Gerald.

The gray dress, besides having the two gashes, now had an L-shaped rip and two bullet holes in the back. The eagle feathers had turned solid white.

Martha's head was reeling. What relationship did any of these three people have with her? To her knowledge, no one in her family had ever mentioned them. Had her husband's name, Davis, once been Degas? Did her family have anything to do with the Tates?

It was now 2025—how many generations had passed since the 1890s?

Everything Martha had experienced left her with a deep sense of unease. She went back down into the house and found a good, strong padlock. Then she returned to the attic and locked the hasp on the trunk.

She decided to let sleeping dogs lie.

POISON

James was trolling the carnival for young women. He knew it sounded bad—*trolling*—but that was exactly what he was doing. This was the best place in this part of the city to meet single young women during the summer. When the carnival came to town, it wasn't unusual to see two or three women in their twenties strolling about with ice cream cones in hand, laughing and talking to each other.

He had had no luck in dating since he and his last girlfriend had broken up. James had visited all the dating services and match sites on the internet. Most of his encounters lasted, on average, two dates. Most of the women he met were, like himself, desperate.

His last date had lasted less than two hours. James ended up driving her home but didn't walk her to the door or even wait to see whether she got into the building safely. He just sped away.

Thursday night wasn't very busy at the carnival. It was slim pickings. He eyed a medium-built blonde, maybe in her late twenties. She wore a sleeveless white cotton dress that fell just below her knees. She was holding a wide-brimmed white straw hat and wore a pair of simple leather sandals. Nothing extraordinary, but there was something about her—her body language, perhaps—that created an aura. She was with a man who appeared to be about her age.

They were at the booth where you throw three baseballs at old-style steel milk bottles. If you managed to knock them all down, you won a huge teddy bear. James wandered over in their direction. As he got closer, he heard the woman say:

"Everette, I don't need a teddy bear. I'm a big girl now."

"Heather, just look at that big, cute white polar bear. I want to take three more chances to win it."

Everette dug into his pocket, paid the carny five dollars, and collected three balls. His first throw narrowly missed the pyramid of bottles. James walked over to the carny and handed over money for three balls. His first throw knocked the bottle off the top of the pyramid.

Neither James nor Everette had any luck with the rest of the balls in their first set. Nor did they succeed in knocking down all the bottles with the next set.

Everette knocked down all the bottles except one with his next three throws. The carny handed him a Kewpie doll as a consolation prize. Before James threw the last ball from his third set, he winked at the carny, leaned over, and deftly slipped a twenty into the man's shirt pocket. Then he threw his last ball, knocking down the remaining four bottles. The carny stepped on a lever that shook the platform, causing all the bottles to fall. James chose the polar bear and walked over to where Everette and Heather were standing.

"Hey, I'll trade you," he said to Everette, who was still holding the Kewpie doll.

"What?" Everette said.

"I'd like to trade you the polar bear for your Kewpie doll. You see, I was just trying to win something for my little niece. When I walked up, I heard you were trying to win this bear for your girlfriend. My niece can't even pick this thing up. If I trade you for the doll, I can give her something she can actually hold."

"Oh no, we can't accept that," Heather said. "Though that's very generous of you, I'm sure your niece will love this bear."

"Yes, but she's only three, and I'm sure my sister will just sit this huge bear in a corner of my niece's room, where it'll stay until my sister has grandchildren—if the house lasts that long."

"I don't know what to say other than thank you," Everette said as he handed over the Kewpie doll and James turned over the bear. "Look, let's walk over to the beer garden so I can buy you a beer."

"Good idea," Heather said. "It's the least we can do. I think I'll have one myself. I'm Heather, and this is my cousin Everette, who's visiting from New York."

"I'm James Darling. Thanks, but you folks don't owe me anything," James said. But he still took them up on their offer.

The three of them sat at a table in the beer garden, drinking cold beer from mugs. James had learned little more about them during the conversation. Heather's last name was Winthrop; Everette's was Walker. Both had grown up in the city. Everette's family had relocated to New York immediately after he finished high school. Heather had lost both of her parents and now lived in a ritzy suburb called Pepper Pike.

Everette and James finished a couple of beers, while Heather sipped on one the whole time they were there. Afterwards, they said their good-byes outside the beer garden and went their separate ways.

James passed by the booth where they had been throwing balls earlier and gave the carny another twenty. He knew the man—Skip. Skip had been with the carnival for about eight years and came through the city every year. James had even drawn customers for him for two or three years by pretending to win easily. Everything but the rides in a carnival was a grift.

For the next few days, Heather was on James's mind. He wondered if he would ever get the chance to see her again. What was he thinking? Had he forgotten why he was at the carnival in the first place? From the moment she'd said, *This is my cousin*, he should have done his best to get some form of future contact—her phone number, email address, something!

James pulled into the parking lot of his neighborhood supermarket. When he reached the front door, he found a sign stating that the store had been closed by the Department of Health. Good, he thought. They should have closed it long ago. He never bought anything fresh from that store, and anything he did buy had to be packaged with an expiration date stamped on it. Now he knew why there were only two cars in the parking lot.

The only bad thing was that he had to drive another ten blocks just to shop—when all he needed were a couple of jars of spaghetti sauce, spaghetti, and some garlic bread. He was in an aisle of a Win-Rite Supermarket, searching for his favorite sauce, when he looked up and saw the manager coming out of the back office behind a young woman holding some papers. Heather!

James watched the pair head straight for produce. Heather was talking to the manager, waving the papers and making broad gestures with her arms.

James started walking toward produce but stayed at a distance from the manager and Heather. When they began heading back to the office, he made sure their paths would intersect.

"Heather?"

"James! How are you doing? This is a surprise." Heather waved the manager off, and he continued toward the office.

"I've been doing pretty well. What are you—the manager's manager?"

Heather let out a small laugh. "Is there even such a thing? No, I'm the owner."

"Oh, you own this Win-Rite?"

"No—all five of them. My grandfather, the founder, started with one store. He incorporated our family name, Winthrop, when he named it Win-Rite. My father and uncle eventually expanded it. My uncle died years ago, then his wife, and they had no children. I lost my parents last year. No siblings. So now I'm the only one."

"You've got a big job. You handling it okay?"

"My father must have seen this coming. He encouraged me to get an MBA from the University of Pennsylvania. Say, I'm glad we ran into each other. I was thinking about you the other day, wondering if I'd ever see you again."

"Same here."

"So why don't we have dinner sometime?"

"Whoa—are you asking me out on a date?"

"Come on now, you can't be surprised in this day and age if a woman asks you out."

"No, of course not. What's your number? I'll text you."

Heather sat at the manager's desk and shuffled through some papers. Afterwards, she handwrote a long memo to the manager and attached it to the stack. She couldn't help but think of Mr. James Darling. She thought he was handsome enough—dark hair, about six feet three, medium build—like maybe he had spent some time in a gym. But talking to him at the carnival and just now, he seemed a little parochial, like maybe he'd been born and raised in the city and had never left. Some people are like that: they spend their whole lives here and die here, without ever setting foot outside the city. James was very different from the men she usually dealt with. They were all cookie-cutter types she had known since she was a debutante. They'd all gone to Ivy League schools and were now either working in the stock market or co-chairing one of their fathers' companies. James was different. He didn't have a preppy way of dressing and acted like he had more street culture.

James put his groceries away and thought about taking Heather out to dinner. It couldn't be just any place—this woman was high society. Maybe she'd like that new French restaurant across town—the one that served snails. You don't meet this type of woman on the internet. This woman wore a Rolex and drove a Jaguar. He, on the other hand, was a nursing assistant with an associate degree and a city certification, driving a Toyota.

James left late for his date with Heather on purpose. He wanted to see if he could get a rise out of her—to see how she'd respond. However, when he rang her bell, she answered quickly. She was already dressed and didn't invite him inside.

"I'm ready," she said, and stepped out, closing the door behind her.

James opened the car door, and Heather slid in. He got in on the driver's side and drove off.

"Where are we going?" Heather asked.

"I have a surprise for you—I think you'll enjoy it. I'll give you a hint: it's Asian."

Heather's thoughts immediately went to the new Vietnamese restaurant that had opened about a month ago. But she'd already been there, and that wouldn't be a surprise—though James didn't know that, she thought. Now it seemed James was driving in a different direction. They ended up just outside the city, in front of a Chinese restaurant she had never seen before.

James and Heather went inside and were seated by the waiter, who handed them a one-sheet menu. It featured photos of dishes with what appeared to be three or four dumplings on each. At the bottom of each photo was a small box.

"Dim Sum," James began. "It's the way the Chinese were cooking two thousand years ago, when there were no pots, pans, or woks. They stuff these dumplings with a variety of meats, spices, and vegetables, then place them into a bamboo tray with holes in the bottom, set the tray over boiling water, and steam-cook the dumplings. You choose how many you want from each photo, read a brief description of what it is, and write the number you want in that little box below the picture."

They brought Dim Sum after Dim Sum. James and Heather ate and talked about their early lives and the environments they had grown up in, which were strikingly different. They talked about work, business, and the fun episodes each had experienced in life. Light conversation continued as James drove Heather home.

"I had a wonderful time, James; this really was a surprise."

As James reached to open his car door so he could open Heather's she stopped him.

"No, James—don't get out of the car. It's raining, and I have an umbrella in my purse. I'm good. Call me."

With that, she leaned over and kissed him on the cheek, then dashed to her front door under her umbrella. James watched her until she entered the house, then drove off.

Once inside, Heather reflected on the evening. It had been a long time since she'd enjoyed the company of a man. She looked forward to seeing James again.

After just a few dates, Heather and James seemed to hit it off. Within six months, they were finishing each other's sentences and making spontaneous, synchronized remarks. Heather took James to places he had never been in the city.

She introduced him to the city's most exclusive club, where she held a lifetime membership. At golf, James was just a duffer, but Heather played well. She took him to a polo match, and they sat ringside at every major boxing match in town. Her company even had a skybox at the football stadium.

Within eight months, they were engaged. They went to Hawaii to celebrate and were married the following year, spending their honeymoon in Paris.

By that time, James was working only a couple of days a week at the hospital. He had grown accustomed to Heather's wealth. There were moments when he couldn't help but think of dollar signs whenever he looked at her.

He now helped her with anything she needed at the stores. Whenever he needed money, he simply took it from one of the store's receipts—but he reported it, and Heather always knew how much it was. The only reason he still worked at the hospital was because he wanted income that wasn't tied to Win-Rite Foods.

Allie Westcott sat on the screened-in porch of her newly purchased two-bedroom Craftsman-style home. It overlooked a modest but thoughtfully designed garden. She reflected on how this house wouldn't have been possible three years ago. Back then, she had been a pole dancer at a gentlemen's club.

But through her friend Martha, she met a bold and charismatic woman named Pamela Hayes, who was running for state senator in her district. Martha recruited her as a volunteer for Pamela's campaign. After all, Allie worked with a lot of people at the club and was free most days to knock on doors.

Allie worked her way up to coordinator in the campaign office. Pamela won the election, and now Allie had the pleasure of serving as her chief of staff.

She was thumbing through the *Daily Herald*, sipping a cup of her favorite Earl Grey tea, when she saw a marriage announcement in the Society section: one of the city's biggest socialites, Miss Heather Winthrop, heir to the Win-Rite Foods chain, had gotten married.

That wasn't surprising. What was surprising was the man beside her in the photo—the groom. He was the father of Allie's two-year-old son.

Heather had been busy all week planning a luncheon and forum to raise money for Children First, an organization that cared for foster children and provided shelters for those in the state's custody.

For the luncheon, Pamela Hayes—who had won election as state senator for District 12 the previous year—would serve as the keynote speaker. Pamela had defeated the incumbent, a homophobic misogynist who had held the seat for two terms.

The luncheon cost five hundred dollars per plate; the forum was free. Most of the attendees would be businesswomen from districts across the state—CEOs, CFOs, and presidents of both small and large companies. Representatives from civil rights and women's organizations would also be present, along with a few men.

Heather turned to James, who was helping her set up the seating and organize the kitchen.

"Do you think this hall is big enough?" she asked.

"Well, you've got seating at the tables for one hundred fifty. You sent out invitations for two hundred—how many RSVPs did you get?"

"One hundred twenty-two."

"Accounting for any stragglers, I'd say we've got more than enough."

James was outside the hall when Pamela Hayes arrived from the hotel. On the day of the luncheon, he served as Heather's liaison with the staff so she could act fully as hostess and emcee.

The driver exited the limousine and rushed around to open the door for Senator Hayes. She stepped out in a gray linen summer dress with a matching waist-length jacket.

Behind her, carrying a small briefcase in one hand and sheaves of papers and pamphlets in the other, was Allie—James's ex-girlfriend.

He didn't notice her at first, focused as he was on the senator. But when his eyes finally landed on Allie, he nearly passed out.

She looked different. Her hair was cut short and styled with a textured look. She appeared more businesslike now. She wore a two-piece beige cotton pantsuit, a white blouse, and tan wedge-heeled shoes. And she wore glasses. His eyes followed her across the hall to the dais, where she sat in a chair next to Pamela Hayes.

He didn't want her to see him just yet, so he slipped away to the kitchen to check on the caterers.

Over the next two hours, however, their eyes met a couple of times. Allie didn't seem surprised—and didn't act as if she recognized him.

They finally came face to face after the forum, when the senator was led to the table of the event's host and hostess.

Senator Hayes introduced Allie to James and Heather as her chief of staff. They all shook hands and exchanged pleasantries.

While dessert was being served, Pamela Hayes circulated between the tables, shaking as many hands as she could. Allie followed her, snapping photos as Pamela cozied up to some of the big shots.

James had no opportunity to speak to Allie alone, but she slipped him a business card before she left. He noticed that she had written another number on the back.

James sat in the office of one of the Win-Rite supermarkets, collecting current data, reviewing deliveries, and gathering cash and receipts to deposit at the bank. He pulled Allie's business card from his wallet and studied the front:

"Allie B. Westcott, Chief of Staff to Pamela Hayes, State Senator, District 12."

A small phrase was printed in tiny letters: *Together we stand, divided we fall.*

He smiled, wondering if that was the district's motto—or just something Allie had borrowed from *The Three Musketeers.*

He and Allie had shared some good times. But those moments were often interrupted by her constant hints about marriage—things like, "You know, two can live cheaper than one," or, "People who live alone don't live as long as those who live with someone."

At the time, he had just been certified as a nursing assistant, and Allie was working as a stripper. He had nothing, and so did she. Two nothings together only made a bigger nothing.

Besides, he had just turned thirty, and marriage was the farthest thing from his mind.

Plus, he thought, why buy the cow when you can get the milk for free?

Eventually, he broke things off with Allie.

He picked up the phone and dialed the number on the back of the card.

"Hello?"

"Hey, Allie—it's James. How's everything?"

"Oh, James, I'm glad you called. I didn't see any point in letting people know we knew each other at the fundraiser last week and having to explain how."

"Good idea—avoids all the questions. You looked really different; I almost didn't recognize you."

"Well, a lot has changed. I want to tell you how my life suddenly turned around—and introduce you to the one who made that happen.

Look, I've got a place not far from Brunswick. Why don't you come over for lunch this week? We can talk then."

"Okay—Thursday's clear for me. If that works, just text me your address."

"Fine. I'll see you then."

When James pulled up in front of Allie's house, he found it small, quaint, and situated on a large lot—landscaped, he was sure, by a professional.

It was certainly a far cry from Heather's family home in Pepper Pike, with its seven bedrooms, six and a half baths, indoor pool, and servant quarters.

Allie's place had curb appeal, but it didn't seem to reflect her personality—not the way he remembered it.

He went to the door and used the knocker—there was no bell.

Allie opened it and waved him in with a smile.

"On time? Now *that's* a change," she said.

"There've been a lot of changes—for both of us."

"Sure you're right. I've got broiled salmon, macaroni and cheese, and pickled beets. Still one of your favorites?"

"It sure is. I haven't had it in years."

A young boy emerged from the back of the house and ran up to Allie, holding a deflated plastic ball.

"Mama, Mama—my ball went down!"

"Don't worry, sweetheart—we'll blow it back up."

Allie turned to James. "This is the person I wanted you to meet—the one who made the biggest change in my life. James Darling, meet Byron James Westcott. He's three years old."

James offered his hand; the boy shook it firmly.

He stared into the child's face, a thousand thoughts racing through his mind. Allie's father was named Byron—and the boy bore James's own name as well.

Looking at the boy was like looking in a mirror. If you compared one of James's childhood photos to Byron's face now, you wouldn't be able to tell the difference.

He began mentally calculating: the last time he'd been with Allie... the boy's age... the timing...

"Why don't you go to your room, honey? Mama will be there to blow up your ball in a minute."

The boy walked off to his room.

"He reminds me a lot of myself at that age."

"He should. You're his father."

James found the nearest chair and sat down, his hand pressed to his forehead.

"What?"

"Let me blow up Byron's ball, turn on his TV, and give him some milk and cookies. You can wash up in the half bath and take a seat at the table—I'll be right back."

When Allie returned, she began setting the dishes on the table.

"When was Byron born, Allie?"

"Seven months after we broke up."

"So you knew you were pregnant while we were still together—yet you said nothing?"

Allie spoke as she served James's plate. "James, I admit I was hounding you about getting married. But I didn't want your decision to be based on other circumstances. It should have been based on you feeling the way I felt about you."

"Come on, Allie—what makes you think I didn't feel the same way about you?"

"Well, I believed telling you I was pregnant would have backed you into a corner and forced you to make a decision you didn't truly want.

Last year, I saw in the paper that you'd married socialite and heiress Heather Winthrop, and I thought you might never know you had a son.

Then we met again—by unbelievable coincidence."

Not much was said for the rest of the meal. Allie spoke briefly about her job, but that was all. They washed down the meal with a robust Riesling and finished with double chocolate cake for dessert. Afterward, James said goodbye to Byron, thanked Allie for her hospitality, and left.

James felt unsettled all the way home. *He had a son,* he thought. *He had a son.*

He tried to figure out how this would square with Heather. She had suffered a miscarriage two months earlier, and they were doing their best to conceive again.

To cope with the loss, Heather had thrown herself into civic work. She chaired the board of the opera house, sat on the school board, and served on both the mayor's and the county president's advisory committees.

With all that, plus her role in managing the stores, she and James had little time together to focus on conceiving another baby.

In the months that followed, James told Heather nothing about Allie—or that he had a son with another woman.

He began making occasional visits to Allie's house to see Byron. He brought gifts and toys, read him stories, and helped with simple jigsaw puzzles.

On one of those visits, as the saying goes, one thing led to another. While Byron napped, Allie and James had sex. And just like that, the affair began.

Sometimes they met at her home; other times, they slipped away to a hotel out of town.

This went on for just over a year—and during that time, Heather gave birth to a girl.

Heather paced back and forth in front of the box office at the Civic Opera House. She had tickets for herself and James, and he was supposed to meet her there.

He was late—as he had been several times over the past month. A couple of times, he hadn't shown up at all.

But this was different. It was opening night: a new production of Puccini's *La Bohème*. They had been saving this date for months.

Once the curtain rose, no one would be admitted into the auditorium until intermission. If anyone left during the performance, they wouldn't be allowed back in until then.

With only five minutes remaining, Heather left James's ticket at the box office and made her way to her seat.

When Heather stepped out at intermission, James was standing there in his tuxedo.

She detoured around him and went straight to the refreshment counter.

She ordered a glass of Cabernet, and when she turned around, James was right in front of her.

"James, I don't want to hear another one of your sorry excuses. This has been happening far too often lately. I don't know where you've been or what you've been doing—but we'll talk about it later. You are not going to show up late like this and ruin the opera for me. So go in there, find your seat—I'll join you shortly."

Heather took another sip of her wine and turned a page in her program.

James walked away without a word and entered the auditorium.

One day, Heather finished her business at the stores and came home early. James arrived about thirty minutes later.

He walked through the door wearing his gray Glen plaid suit, a white shirt, and a dark blue paisley tie.

Funny, she thought. *When he left this morning, he was wearing a light blue shirt.*

She didn't think much of it—until two days later, when she asked their part-time butler/chauffeur/handyman, Kenneth, to put a coat of wax on her Jaguar.

Kenneth had trouble finding the wax—it wasn't in the garage.

Heather checked James's Range Rover and found the wax under a tarp in the cargo area. She also found one of James's light blue shirts.

There was a red smudge high on the right side near the shoulder. It looked as if someone had tried to scrub it out. *What was it—ketchup? Blood? Lipstick?*

She found more of the stain farther down the front of the shirt, untouched. If it was lipstick, it wasn't her shade.

Heather was breastfeeding her daughter, Jewel, in the sunroom, enjoying the way the sun sank slowly behind the trees, its brightness gently fading.

She was on maternity leave and had left most of the store operations in James's hands.

About twenty minutes earlier, James had been enjoying the sunroom with her and Jewel, but he'd gone upstairs to shower.

He had left his phone in the wicker chair where he'd been sitting, and it had slipped down beside the cushion. Now, it was ringing.

Heather got up and, with Jewel in one arm, fished the phone out from the chair.

"Hello?"

There was a pause on the other end. "Martha?"

"No, you must have the wrong number."

"Thanks—you didn't sound like her." The woman quickly hung up.

Heather paused. The voice had sounded familiar.

"Who was that?" James asked, walking into the room in a terrycloth bathrobe and drying his hair with a fluffy towel.

"Wrong number," Heather said, handing him his phone.

Weeks later, Heather found herself wondering how James seemed to disappear—sometimes in the middle of the day, sometimes late at night.

He said he'd been doing a lot of out-of-town shopping, meeting with new suppliers and negotiating better prices.

But the hours didn't always make sense. He rarely called her during those times, and when she called him, he usually texted back.

It was during one of those absences that she thought again about the wrong-number phone call.

Nah, she told herself—and then felt almost ashamed for suspecting James of seeing someone else.

But still—one night, she fought the urge to take a closer look at James's phone as it lay on the nightstand beside their bed while he slept.

She shouldn't, she thought. *The basic foundation of a marriage is trust.*

She went back and forth in her head—until finally, she gave in.

She picked up the phone and took it into the next room.

She knew James's passcode. He didn't know she knew it—but she did.

She checked the recent calls on his iPhone. Because she remembered the number from the wrong-number call, she easily spotted it—there were dozens of calls to and from that number, almost daily.

Some were short, two or three minutes; others lasted as long as twenty.

Heather placed the phone back on the nightstand—and did what any self-respecting wife with her resources would do: she hired a private detective the very next day.

Harry Hall was a hefty six-footer, weighing in at two hundred and twenty pounds. He had dark eyes and a receding hairline that stretched all the way to the back of his head. What hair remained around the edges was three inches long and unruly.

He appeared unassuming—average, even—except for his garish plaid sports coat and the Hush Puppies he wore.

He walked into Heather's office finishing off a hot dog, balled up the napkin, and tossed it into the trash can.

Reaching into his jacket pocket, he pulled out a business card, offering it with his left hand while extending his right for a handshake.

Still chewing the last bite of his hot dog, he spoke:

"Harry Hall, Esquire—Star Detective Agency—at your service, ma'am."

Heather looked up at the man standing in front of her. She shook his hand, then shook her head slightly, squinting at his card as he sat down across from her.

She couldn't believe this was the man who ran the top-rated detective agency in the area—the one she'd read about and been referred to by her neighbor, Sarah.

"Heather Darling. Win-Rite Foods," she said, introducing herself.

"Mr. Hall, I'd like to hire you to conduct a thorough and highly confidential investigation of my husband. I don't want any of your assistants or office staff to know. And, of course, my husband must never suspect he's being followed or tracked in any way.

My initial suspicion is infidelity—but I want to be sure."

"Confidentiality is the hallmark of my agency, Mrs. Darling—and I understand why someone in your position values that most.

Only you and I will know the identity of any subjects involved. I'll need a two-thousand-dollar retainer. My fee is two hundred dollars an hour, plus expenses.

I'll update you every three days. Sometimes I may have nothing to report—and in those cases, you'll receive no details until the final report.

If you agree to these terms, please sign this contract."

Harry Hall placed a contract on Heather's desk.

After signing the contract, Heather handed Mr. Hall a piece of paper, a photograph, and a check.

"This paper has the phone number of a woman who's been having frequent conversations with my husband. Start by finding out who she is.

The photo is of my husband—James Darling."

Two weeks later, Mr. Hall returned to Heather's office with a portfolio full of documents and photographs.

There were records of times and dates, hotel receipts, bank statements, and recent purchases. He had addresses, work history, and social connections going back six years.

Hall billed Heather for thirty hours—totaling $6,500, including expenses.

She wrote him a check, subtracting the retainer, and Mr. Hall left as quickly as he had arrived.

Heather sat at her desk, materials spread out in front of her.

Harry Hall had left her everything—not just documents and photos, but also video and audio recordings.

But what shocked her beyond belief was discovering that the woman James had been linked to was Allie—the Chief of Staff to State Senator Pamela Hayes.

The documents showed that Allie Westcott was thirty-two years old and lived in Brunswick with her four-year-old son.

There were photos of Allie and James together—in her car, in his car, entering hotels, dining at restaurants.

There were pictures of them in nearly every situation imaginable, except in bed.

There were even photos of James with Allie and her son.

What Heather couldn't understand was how James and Allie had developed such a deep relationship after supposedly meeting just last year.

That mystery was short-lived. When she read the social history on each of them, she discovered they had known each other for more than five years.

Heather was devastated. Had she been duped from the beginning?

If anyone had told her this before, she would have sworn it wasn't true—but here it was, laid out in full, documented and undeniable.

She crumpled into her chair and wept for what felt like an hour.

Armed with the information, Heather went to her neighbor Sarah, whom she had known since childhood.

Sarah was fifteen years older, had once been married, but lost her husband to cancer. She'd never had children, but had babysat Heather during her teenage years.

Heather trusted Sarah completely. She knew she could ask for personal advice without fear that anything they discussed would be passed along to others in her social circle.

She asked for a referral to a divorce lawyer, and Sarah gave her two names. Heather didn't share any details, and Sarah didn't press her.

Heather stood at the kitchen counter, pouring herself a glass of wine.

Her back was to the family room, where James reclined on the chaise lounge reading the newspaper.

"I tried calling you three times this afternoon, and you didn't return a single one. What kept you so busy that you couldn't call me back?" Heather asked.

James swung his feet off the chaise lounge and sat up, folding the newspaper shut.

"I'm sorry, sweetheart, but I was in Kent with a potential new vendor. The owner gave me a tour of his cold storage.

You know how those walk-in reefers are—you can't get a signal inside.

I saw your calls when I came out, but I got wrapped up in other discussions and just plain forgot."

He rose, walked over, and hugged her from behind.

"Forgive me this time, honey. I won't be so distracted again that I forget to return your call."

"Are you sure you weren't in Brunswick at 338 Park Drive?"

"What are you talking about?"

Heather lied—she didn't want James to know just yet how much she already knew.

"Someone told me they saw your Range Rover parked in a driveway at that address a couple of weeks ago. Your Range Rover—with your vanity plates."

"Now wait a minute. Whoever told you that is lying."

"Maybe. But I did some checking and found out the house belongs to Allie Westcott—Chief of Staff to Senator Pamela Hayes. I didn't realize you two already knew each other when Pamela introduced her to us at the luncheon."

"Well, let me come clean, Heather. I've been meaning to tell you. Yes, Allie and I were involved years ago. When we saw each other at the luncheon, it had been years since we last spoke. Neither of us thought it was worth mentioning—we're living different lives now, and neither of us wanted to muck things up."

"You didn't want to muck things up? Well, now you have."

"When we reconnected, Allie told me she was seven months pregnant when we broke up. She has a three-year-old son—and I'm the father. When I found out, I wanted to tell you, but it was right after your miscarriage. I was afraid it would only make things worse. I've just been visiting my son from time to time—that's all that's been going on."

"Oh, come off it, James! I may be surprised you have a son—but were you visiting him on May 20th, when you and Allie checked into the Rainbow Motel on Route 71?"

"What? Where did you get that information?"

"Drop it. Just drop it, James. You say you want to come clean, but listen to yourself—you're more concerned with figuring out how I found out than actually explaining anything."

"Well, you're coming at me with all this half-baked information, and I just want to set the record—"

"Half-baked, you say? You should assume I know everything. My miscarriage was nearly a year ago, and I gave birth to Jewel over two months ago. You've had plenty of time to tell me you have a son. But actually, this isn't about your son—it's about you and Allie."

"Okay, okay, okay. Allie and I may have met up once or twice—and yes, I gave in to weakness. We had sex. But it didn't mean anything—"

"What about four times in the last two weeks?" Heather interrupted, arms crossed, her expression defiant.

James's jaw dropped.

"Look, James—this thing between us isn't going to be mended like this, if it can be mended at all. Not when you keep lying. You can't even face what you've done. And I bet it's been going on since the very beginning. I can't stand to be near you right now. Find another bedroom to sleep in tonight."

"Now wait just a minute!"

"The alternative, James, is that I call our little police department here in Pepper Pike—where long-standing residents are always given deference. My grandfather helped found this community. If I tell them I want you out of this house, they'll waste no time in removing you—physically, if necessary."

James reluctantly packed a few things into a small duffel bag and went down the hall to the first guest bedroom.

The nursery adjoined the master bedroom. Heather locked the outer doors to both rooms and prepared for bed.

Surprisingly, her emotions didn't lead her to tears, as they might have before.

What was it Camus said? she thought. *What doesn't kill me makes me stronger.*

And she did feel stronger.

That first confrontation between Heather and James was mild compared to the knock-down, drag-out fights that followed.

Some days, they moved through the house without saying a single word to each other.

On the days they did speak, it was through vicious personal attacks—name-calling, admonishments, and outright humiliation.

The word *divorce* didn't come up until the fourth argument. But when it did, it triggered a definitive shift in James's demeanor.

At the mere mention of it, he slammed on the brakes—mentally—and began scrambling to reverse course.

He had signed a prenuptial agreement. If he left, he'd take only what he could carry on his back or load into his Range Rover.

And he certainly couldn't survive on his two-day-a-week hospital job.

He loved his daughter, Jewel, deeply and shared a remarkably close bond with her. No matter what happened, he refused to give up custody.

Over the next two weeks, James and Heather walked on eggshells around each other.

They exchanged greetings and polite conversation, both carefully avoiding the elephant in the room.

But beneath the surface, something simmered.

By this time, James had begun to grapple with how it all might end.

A number of scenarios ran through his head.

Had Heather seen a lawyer yet?

Maybe he could claim alimony.

If the marriage ended in divorce, perhaps he could keep living in a separate part of the house.

But the most plausible—and worry-free—solution, he thought, was for Heather to have an accident.

Aside from the two days a week he still worked at the hospital, James hadn't given up helping Heather with the stores.

But with his marriage in limbo and almost no interaction with his children, he hadn't been sleeping well.

Those thoughts weighed heavily on his mind one afternoon as he worked in the ER, assisting a nurse who had just finished bandaging a patient.

She was called to the front—two gurneys were on the way in.

One of the other nurses had left open a cabinet that held various ER medical supplies.

As James passed, he reflexively grabbed one of the 100-milliliter insulin pens.

He turned it over in his hand, toying with the idea of what he could do with it.

The next week, James convinced Heather that they should spend an evening together—no talk of their situation. Just a board game or a movie.

They sat down to play Spades, listened to a new Diana Krall recording, and kept the conversation light—mostly about Jewel, how James could spend more time with her, and the goings-on at the stores.

"I'm going to get a drink. Want me to bring you anything?"

"Yes, bring me a glass of wine," Heather replied.

James walked over to the bar cabinet and poured himself a double shot of bourbon. Then he poured Heather a glass of wine.

From his pocket, he pulled a napkin, unfolded it, and retrieved two Ativan tablets he'd stolen from her bottle on the dresser.

He crushed the pills and stirred the powder into her wine.

Returning to the card table, he handed her the glass as he sat down.

She took a sip. A small frown crossed her face as she looked at the glass—but she said nothing.

They played a few more hands. Heather was on a winning streak.

She drank more wine. By the fourth hand, she was feeling drowsy.

She raised the back of her hand to her forehead and leaned back in her chair.

"Are you okay, honey?"

"I'm feeling woozy, I…"

"Here, let me help you to your room. Maybe if you lie down for a bit."

James helped Heather from her chair, draping her arm around his neck. With one hand holding hers and the other around her waist, he guided her upstairs.

After laying her on the bed and making her comfortable, he left the room to retrieve the insulin pen from his own.

Heather didn't stir as her clothes were rearranged.

But when she felt a sting in her abdomen, she blinked, disoriented, and through the blur saw James standing over her—holding a pen-like object with a sharp point.

She fought to keep her eyes open, but they slowly closed.

James knew it would take time for the insulin to trigger hypoglycemia and have its fatal effect.

He went downstairs, washed the glasses, and put away the cards.

Then he broke the insulin pen into pieces and shoved them down the garbage disposal.

When he returned upstairs, he checked Heather's pulse—nothing.

James pulled her from the bed and laid her on the floor, mimicking the proper position for CPR.

Only then did he call 911.

When the EMTs arrived, James lied. He told them he'd found his wife unresponsive on the bed, dragged her to the floor, and attempted to revive her.

One of the paramedics, kneeling beside Heather, said loudly, "I've got a pulse!"

"What?" James shouted. "You've got a pulse?"

"Yeah. It's faint—but it's there," the medic said, placing an oxygen mask over her face.

"You've got to get her to a hospital—now!"

"Jerry, give me a hand," the paramedic said to his partner.

"Let's get her on the gurney—we'll evaluate her more in the ambulance.

Mister, you'll ride with us. We've got some questions for you, and I'm sure the hospital staff will too."

The doctor approached James in the waiting room.

"Mr. Darling, your wife is in a hypoglycemic coma. She has an excessive amount of insulin in her system. Is she diabetic?"

"No. Neither of us is diabetic."

"Well then, walk me through the events of this evening. How did you end up here at the hospital with your wife?"

"I came home from the Win-Rite store on Clayborn, and Heather greeted me at the door. She immediately said she was going upstairs to lie down—said she felt a little tired.

I turned on the TV and watched the local news. About an hour later, I went up to my room to get a book. As I passed Heather's room, I called out to her—just softly—but she didn't answer, so I figured she was still napping."

"Okay."

"But about forty minutes later, I went into her room and shook her—but there was no response.

I shook her again and started calling her name.

I checked her pulse and didn't feel one. So I laid her on the floor and started CPR.

When I still couldn't get a response, I called 911."

"Strange that you didn't get a response while doing CPR. Maybe she'd already lapsed into the coma."

"I thought she was gone. When the paramedic said he found a pulse, I was shocked. It pulled me back from the horror of what I thought was the worst moment of my life."

"Is there any insulin in the house?"

"No—and when I came home, I didn't see any hypodermic needles or insulin.

When I found her in the bedroom, there were no signs of anything. Can't you bring her out of the coma?"

"We can induce a coma—but bringing someone out of one is something medicine has yet to master.

We'll treat her hypoglycemia and wait. That's all we can do."

"Can I see her now?"

"She's still in a coma, with no change since her arrival—but yes, you can see her.

This officer will accompany you home afterward," the doctor added, nodding to a policeman in the corridor.

James stepped into the room and saw Heather lying peacefully, still and pale.

Then he exited and approached the officer.

"Sir, if your wife isn't diabetic, then she was either poisoned or attempted suicide," Officer O'Neal said.

"In either case, there may be evidence in your home that you haven't noticed. I might find something that helps us understand what happened."

James opened the front door, and he and Officer O'Neal, along with the officer's partner, stepped inside.

James greeted Cynthia—the neighbor's teenage daughter—whom he had called from the hospital to check on Jewel.

He now called her parents to let her mother know she was heading home.

The first place James led the officers was Heather's bedroom.

He then stepped into the adjoining nursery to check on Jewel.

The officers examined every corner of the bedroom: they looked under the bed, through the covers, in the en suite bathroom, both nightstands, across the floor with a flashlight, and even through the contents of the trash can.

When Officer O'Neal opened the closet, he turned to James.

"Sir, I don't see any of your clothes in here. The two of you don't share this room?"

"No—my room is down the hall," James replied.

After sweeping through Jewel's room, the officers made their way down the hall to James's bedroom.

They searched it thoroughly, along with the adjoining bathroom.

Then they moved downstairs, conducting a cursory search of the living room, dining room, and kitchen.

They also sifted through the kitchen garbage.

In the end, they left the house empty-handed.

The next day, James decided that one of the store's managers would take over both his and Heather's duties. Devin Lloyd—a dependable man who had been with Win-Rite Foods for nearly thirty years—was chosen.

James also hired a professional live-in nanny, Amy Beckham, to care for Jewel.

There was a bedroom for her on the first floor, outfitted with a monitor to receive video and audio from Jewel's room.

James intended to spend most of his time at the hospital with Heather.

He wanted to be there if she ever came out of the coma.

He couldn't risk the possibility that she might regain consciousness, remember what happened before she slipped under, and tell someone.

She had looked directly at him while he was still holding the pen—and he'd already told EMTs and hospital staff that he was never in the room while she was conscious.

"What do you mean you can't put another bed in this room?" James asked the floor nurse, referring to Heather's room in case he wanted to stay overnight.

"Mr. Darling, we can provide you with a cot, but we have single rooms and double rooms. Single rooms get one bed; double rooms get two. Your wife is in a single."

"Right—and we should be permitted to have anything in that room we want. We're not intruding on anyone's space or privacy."

"I'm sorry, Mr. Darling. That's hospital policy—it's not up to me."

James stepped away from the nurse and made a call on his phone.

Two minutes later, he asked the nurse for her name and repeated it into the receiver—then handed her the phone.

"He wants to talk to you."

The nurse took the phone and spoke with Chief Physician Dr. Raymond Flores.

She was told to locate a bed in Lower Level Storage and have someone from Maintenance bring it up—complete with bedding—so Mr. Darling could stay overnight in his wife's room.

James was almost certain his demands would be met.

After all, Heather's father had an entire wing named after him at Holy Child Hospital for contributions he alone had made.

Her family had supported the hospital for more than eighty years—documented and publicized.

With his duties at the stores now limited, James also gave up the two days he worked at Resurrection Hospital.

The staff understood—he didn't offer many details. He simply said that Heather had collapsed in his arms, fallen into a coma, and that doctors were still searching for a cause.

Now, he spent most of his time either at the hospital with Heather, at home, or at Allie's.

He split his time between Jewel, Heather, and Byron.

He and Allie had suspended their rendezvous, and James gave her no hint that he had played any role in Heather's condition.

Hell, he thought, *I didn't do this to be with Allie—I did it to preserve my way of life.*

James stood in the kitchen, helping Allie put away groceries.

"So, the doctors don't know how she ended up in a coma? Not a stroke? Not a heart attack?" Allie asked.

"No. Hypoglycemia—from an insulin overdose. I just don't see how that's possible.

There were no vials or hypodermic needles in the bedroom.

She said she was tired and went straight upstairs to lie down as I came in.

The police went through the house and didn't find anything either."

"Well, why do you spend so much time at the hospital? I mean, she's in a coma—there's nothing you can do for her. And sleeping there—don't you think that's going a little too far?"

"I want to be there when she wakes up. I don't want her to open her eyes and only see strangers. She should see someone she knows. She's got no one. Her aunt Sophia and her son, Everette, came from New York, but they could only stay a few days."

Unfortunately for James, he wasn't at the hospital when Heather came out of her coma—he was at home, eating lunch.

A nurse called him, and he dashed out of the house, leaving half his meal untouched on the plate.

He sped toward the hospital, nearly colliding with two cars along the way.

A hundred thoughts ran through his mind.

Could she talk? Was she asking questions? Did she remember what happened before the coma?

Was her body responding? Could she sit up? Walk?

When James reached Heather's floor, he stepped off the elevator.

As he rounded the corner past the nurses' station, he could see straight through the open door of Heather's room.

As he drew closer, he saw a doctor and a nurse inside.

When he entered the room, Dr. Daniels greeted him and pulled him aside.

Heather lay in bed, staring at the ceiling.

"She came out of her coma about forty minutes ago," Dr. Daniels said.

"It was quiet—we might not have noticed, but one of the nurses saw her eyes open while emptying the catheter bag. We haven't had a response from her yet. Maybe you can get closer, make some physical contact—see if you can reach her."

James walked over and pulled a chair up beside Heather's bed.

He sat down and took her hand.

"Hey, sweetheart—you've been asleep for a long time. It's about time you woke up. How are you feeling?"

Heather didn't turn her head or make eye contact.

James leaned in until they were face to face, but she showed no emotion—no change in expression.

"She's exhibiting sporadic seizures, and when they occur, she lapses into convulsions."

"Well, Dr. Daniels, I'll be staying overnight and will continue trying to communicate with her."

The doctor had connected Heather to a feeding tube.

Over the next few weeks, her therapy consisted of elevating her bed to a sitting position and attempting to feed her solid food—if pudding could be called that.

When the bed was raised, Heather would sit staring straight ahead.

When James stood at the foot of the bed, she would focus on him—but it was as if she were looking through him.

Throughout this time, Heather's demeanor never changed.

She continued to stare through people or off into the distance.

One day, as James arrived on the floor, the nurses' station was empty.

When he got within earshot of Heather's room, he heard something that stopped him in his tracks.

"Can you hear what I'm saying, honey? Try blinking your eyes if you can hear me. Okay—good. Now blink once for yes, twice for no. Do you know where you are? Honey, try blinking again to answer me. Can you try blinking at all?"

James stepped into the room and saw that a nurse was trying to communicate with Heather.

"Oh—Mr. Darling," the nurse said, turning toward him.

"We tried Mrs. Darling with some soft foods, just a spoonful of three different things.

Today's therapy was focused on trying to get her to respond to verbal cues or sounds."

"Any luck?"

"No. I've been trying to get her to respond with her eyes—but so far, only random blinks."

James glanced at Heather and thought he saw her eyes shift in his direction.

The nurse's attempt to communicate had set something in motion.

Now James knew he would have to double his efforts to ensure Heather never revealed what had happened to her.

James began by stealing the identity of a stock boy at one of the Win-Rite Foods stores.

He acquired a fake ID using a disguise and the stock boy's name—Franklin Holder.

Then he secured a credit card under that alias, which allowed him to walk into an internet café and use one of their computers as Franklin Holder.

James found a discreet chemical company and ordered arsenic.

He had it delivered under his false identity to the headquarters office of Win-Rite Foods, Chemical Division—his own office.

Heather's physical condition had been deteriorating for weeks, and Dr. Daniels told James he should hope for the best but prepare for the worst.

James figured it would come as no surprise if Heather suddenly took a downturn and died.

He returned to the internet café to research the dosage of arsenic needed to cause death.

He couldn't afford to repeat his earlier mistake by administering too little to be fatal—but he also didn't want her death to come too quickly.

James determined that the pump controlling Heather's G-tube released two ounces of food per hour from the feeding bag.

He had to calculate the dosage and timing precisely—so he could be home at least thirty minutes before the poison took effect.

His research showed that one gram of arsenic could kill the average adult within two to four hours.

On the day James brought the arsenic to the hospital, he kept a close eye on the feeding tube, watching for the moment the pump would start.

He settled in with a book he had brought.

A nurse came in, adjusted Heather's bed to a sitting position, and stood at the foot of the bed holding up enlarged photographs—trying to elicit a response by watching her facial expressions.

She also tried verbal cues and sounds.

Eventually, the nurse left without disrupting James's timing.

Just after she exited, James slipped the arsenic into Heather's feeding bag.

Then he left the hospital, making sure the nurse on duty saw him go, and started for home.

James was about five minutes from home when his phone rang—it was the hospital.

"Hello?"

The voice on the other end was clear and urgent.

"Mr. Darling, you need to return to the hospital immediately. Your wife has just experienced a grave episode."

"Yes—yes, certainly."

James turned the car around and sped back to the hospital.

His first thought: *It's too soon—I just left.*

He began to panic. Had they discovered his plan? Had someone found the arsenic?

When he arrived, he found Dr. Daniels and a nurse inside Heather's room.

The nurse was dismantling the medical equipment—including Heather's feeding bag and tube—which were immediately discarded.

To James's relief, they were gone.

Dr. Daniels began, "She expired not long after you left. I just happened to be on the floor when we got the code blue. Nurse Clark and I rushed in and found her convulsing—then she fell still."

"But how, Doc? I was just here. She seemed perfectly fine when I left."

"Well, I tried to prepare you for this possibility the other day. Her vitals have been deteriorating—especially over the last four days. It's just... I've never seen someone go out like this."

"What do you mean?"

"I mean the level of seizures and convulsions she experienced. We'll be transferring her to the morgue on the lower level. You'll need to contact them to make arrangements for when and by whom she'll be collected."

"Thanks, Doctor. Can you give me a few minutes alone with her?"

The nurse and Dr. Daniels left the room.

James walked over to Heather, took her hand, and kissed her on the forehead.

He whispered, "I'm truly sorry, Heather."

But as he murmured his version of an apology into her ear, his mind was elsewhere—already racing.

He needed to get her cremated as soon as possible.

Only afterward did he consider notifying her remaining relatives in New York.

Then there was the memorial service to arrange—and informing the Win-Rite employees.

Maybe he'd give them a half day off for mourning and pay them for a full one.

The memorial service was held in a small chapel in Pepper Pike.

Uncle Dave, Aunt Sophia, Everette, and his younger sister, Lois, attended.

A few managers, cashiers, and other Win-Rite Foods employees were also present.

James had arranged framed photographs of Heather beside a hand-painted, cobalt-blue cremation urn.

A looped PowerPoint presentation played, chronicling her cotillion, graduation, and other milestones from her life.

About three days after the memorial service, James came home from the stores and opened the day's mail, which the nanny had left on the office desk.

Among the envelopes was one curious letter addressed to him—his address typed, no return address.

Inside was a note, the message assembled from letters cut from magazines and newspapers:

I know what you did.

For Christ's sake, he thought. *Who sends a letter like this? Sure—on TV and in the movies—but not in real life.*

Just as he was pondering the letter, the phone rang.

Caller ID displayed: *Blake and Hancock Law Office.*

Nervously, he answered. "Hello?"

"Yes, hello—am I speaking with Mr. James Darling?"

"Yes, this is he."

"Well, Mr. Darling, our firm—Blake and Hancock—has on file the will of your late wife, Heather Darling. I'm Franklin Hancock, and I've been named executor of that will.

I'm calling to inform you that the reading is scheduled for next Wednesday, May 4, at 2:00 p.m., at our offices located at 337 Banneker Boulevard.

Subjects in the will, aside from yourself, include your daughter Jewel, Heather's aunt Sophia Walker, and her cousin Everette. All are expected to be present."

"Thank you, Mr. Hancock. Jewel and I will be there."

James was surprised to hear of a will—one he knew nothing about.

When he'd first seen the caller ID, he'd assumed it was a divorce lawyer.

When James arrived at the offices of Blake and Hancock with Jewel and her nanny, Amy Beckham, Aunt Sophia and Everette were already there.

They all took seats in front of Mr. Hancock's desk.

"Since we're all here, I believe we can begin," Hancock said.

James only half listened to the formal introduction of the will—*Being of sound mind and body... blah, blah, blah... on this date, witnessed by...*

He waited patiently for Hancock to get to the meat of it.

"I bequeath to my daughter, Jewel, my total business interest in Win-Rite Foods and full ownership of the house and property in Pepper Pike.

Her father—and my husband—James Darling, is to act as primary custodian of the business and estate.

He will serve as CEO of Win-Rite Foods at a salary of $150,000 per year, adjusted annually for cost of living.

My aunt, Sophia Walker, shall serve as secondary custodian and is bequeathed a one-time sum of $200,000, along with my Mercedes-Benz.

To her son, Everette, I bequeath my Jaguar."

Two days after the will reading, James received another letter—again with no return address.

Like the first, it was crafted from cut-out letters.

This one read:

You think you got away with it.

James now took the letters very seriously.

He no longer believed they were idle threats or guesses.

Whoever was sending them knew something.

On a bright, sunny Monday morning, a short, portly woman with cropped, graying hair—appearing to be in her late fifties—walked into the local police station.

She wore a gray, calf-length wool coat and black oxfords. A black hat with a small bow sat atop her head, and she clutched a medium-sized black purse in both hands, held high in front of her.

She approached the female desk sergeant.

"Excuse me—I had a dear friend who passed away recently. She left me a letter to turn over to the police in the event of her death."

"Okay, Ms...?"

"Spears. Gertrude Spears."

"Let me call a detective, Mrs. Spears. He'll take a statement from you and collect the letter," the desk sergeant said as she picked up the phone.

A detective entered through a door at the back of the station.

"Mrs. Spears, I'm Detective Marshall Field. I understand you have a letter for us?"

"Yes."

"Please, follow me to my desk."

Ms. Spears sat in a chair across from Detective Field and pulled a letter from her purse, handing it to him.

He opened it and saw that it was signed by Heather Darling.

The letter stated that if the police were reading it, she was likely no longer alive—and that her husband, James Darling, would almost certainly have had a hand in her death.

She mentioned ongoing conflict in their marriage, particularly over an affair James was having, and said she had contacted a divorce lawyer.

The letter was dated three months prior.

It was vague, lacking specific details—but it was signed.

"You say Heather Darling was a friend of yours?"

"Yes. We've been good friends for years. She died two weeks ago at Holy Child Hospital.

You may have read about it in the papers—she was the owner of Win-Rite Foods. Her maiden name was Winthrop.

She gave me this letter about two and a half months ago and told me to take it to the police if anything happened to her."

"Ms. Spears, this letter implicates her husband in her death. Do you know anything about that?"

"No. I sure don't."

Detective Field handed Mrs. Spears a pad and pen.

"Well, please write down your name, address, and phone number for future contact. We're going to take a look at this."

Sarah Sullivan walked out of the police station and caught a taxi around the corner to take her home.

She sat in the back seat with a small smile on her face, pleased with how smoothly the drop-off had gone.

She had meticulously drafted that letter using notes she'd collected from Heather—studying and mimicking her handwriting.

This letter, she hoped, would do what those anonymous notes to James had failed to: draw him out and shift the police's attention toward him.

She couldn't include details—she didn't know any. But she was certain James had something to do with her friend's death.

She had watched enough forensic shows to know what to avoid.

She wore latex gloves, and she was careful not to lick the envelope.

Sarah had also given the police a false name, address, and phone number—nothing that could be traced back to her.

Detective Field walked over to his partner Grant Holcomb's desk—it was close enough that Holcomb had overheard the entire conversation with the woman calling herself Gertrude Spears.

"What do you think?" Holcomb asked.

"I don't know. It sounds contrived—like something out of a movie.

But we should probably head over to Holy Child Hospital and see what we can learn about Heather Darling's death."

The detectives met with Dr. Daniels and a nurse.

"Mrs. Darling was brought in nearly a month ago," Daniels told them.

"She was in a hypoglycemic coma. Though she came out of it a week later, her condition steadily deteriorated. Her death wasn't unexpected."

"Was an autopsy performed?" Field asked.

"No," Dr. Daniels replied. "We didn't see a reason to. Her body was released to Mr. Darling, who had her cremated."

"What about the husband? Did he seem concerned about her condition—was he supportive?"

Nurse Callie spoke up. "Very. He was here every day, sometimes overnight.

And, actually, Mrs. Darling passed only minutes after Mr. Darling left that day."

The detectives left the hospital with an urgent need to speak to Mr. Darling.

They contacted him and asked that he come to the station for an interview regarding his wife's death.

James agreed—though he was clearly nervous and visibly unsettled at the request.

Field and Holcomb reviewed a report filed by the officer who had searched the Darling residence for insulin or related paraphernalia on the day Heather was hospitalized.

The file also included James's original statement describing how he'd found his wife before making the 911 call.

They had the 911 recording as well.

When James arrived at the station, Detective Holcomb began the questioning.

"We understand you were at the hospital the day your wife passed away. Is that correct?"

"Yes. I was there every day."

"Did the doctor tell you what caused her death?"

"Natural causes, I guess. Dr. Daniels told me a week earlier that her vital organs were failing."

"There was no autopsy. So you had her cremated without knowing exactly what caused her death?

I'd think you'd want to be sure. And you never found out how she ended up in a hypoglycemic coma—correct?"

"Yeah, but I..."

Detective Field leaned forward. "Mr. Darling, the reason we're asking you about the inconsistencies surrounding your wife's hospitalization and death is this: a friend of your wife brought us a letter, allegedly written by her, implicating you in her death."

"What? What friend? What letter?"

Field handed the letter to James, who read it in stunned silence.

"This isn't Heather's handwriting."

"What do you mean? Why do you say that?"

"I mean—it looks like it. But I'm telling you, it's not. If you compare it to her actual handwriting, you'll see the difference."

"Well, this is all we have," Field replied. "We don't have anything to compare it to."

"I do. I have some samples of her handwriting at home."

"Good. Detective Holcomb will follow you and collect it. We'll have our analyst compare the samples."

James led Detective Holcomb to the home office and began rifling through a drawer, pulling out papers and placing them on the desk.

One document caught Holcomb's attention—a receipt from E-Café on Central Avenue, an internet café, dated April 8.

That was just two weeks before Heather Darling's death.

When Holcomb returned to the station with the handwriting sample, he mentioned the café receipt to Field.

"I mean—why would he need to go to the E-Café if he has his personal computer and access to the Win-Rite Foods network?"

Detective Field couldn't think of a reason—unless Darling wanted to browse sites he didn't want traced to his home or office systems.

He and Holcomb grabbed a photo of James Darling and headed to the E-Café.

"I've never seen this man before," the E-Café manager told the detectives, studying the photo. "But he kinda looks like a guy who came in a few weeks ago. That guy had a mustache, wore glasses—and a really bad brown wig."

"Great. This would've been April 8. Can you tell us which computer he used?"

"Our network logs will show which sites were accessed that day and from which IP addresses, but I can't tell you which specific computer he used. And you'll need a warrant to get that information."

The detectives secured a limited warrant, allowing them access only to a list of sites visited from the E-Café on April 8.

They had the department's IT engineer comb through the logs and flag any suspicious activity.

From over two hundred entries, she identified four sites of concern: one selling firearms and ammunition, one selling explosives, a chemical supplier, and one that appeared to be linked to child pornography.

Detectives Field and Holcomb agreed the chemical supplier was their best lead—though they flagged the child pornography site as a secondary concern.

They contacted the chemical company to see if any purchases made on April 8 could be connected to James Darling.

A supervisor at Davies Chemicals, Inc. reviewed the records and found an invoice dated April 8 for a purchase of three grams of arsenic.

It had been shipped to someone named Franklin Holder at Win-Rite Foods, Chemical Division. She also provided an address.

Detectives Holcomb and Field were stunned—their old-school detective work was finally paying off.

But when they returned to the precinct, bad news awaited them: the handwriting on the letter did not match Heather Darling's.

They tracked down the real Franklin Holder and discovered he was a stock boy at one of the Win-Rite stores.

The arsenic, however, had been shipped to Win-Rite's headquarters—under his name.

"We can reasonably link the arsenic to James Darling," Holcomb said, "but proving it ended up in Mrs. Darling's body is another matter.

He had her cremated. We've got nothing physical to connect the dots."

"Oh, on the contrary, my friend," Field replied. "I was watching a science documentary the other night. It explained that arsenic is a heavy metal—it survives cremation. Mr. Darling keeps Heather's cremains in an urn. I saw it in a Daily Herald photo from the memorial service."

"Yeah, I saw it too—when I went to collect the handwriting sample. Cobalt-blue urn. It's sitting on the mantle in his living room."

If getting the warrant for the internet café had been difficult, it was nothing compared to obtaining one for Heather Darling's cremains.

When they presented the warrant to James, he was visibly startled—his eyes widened, and he shook his head in disbelief.

"You people must be insane," James said, looking at Detective Field. "You want to take my wife's ashes?"

"Yes," Field replied. "We're taking them—but they'll be returned intact, in the urn."

James turned toward Detective Holcomb. "And why are you going through my desk?"

Holcomb looked up. "If you read the warrant carefully, Mr. Darling, you'll see it includes any evidence of poison purchases. Oh, what do we have here? A state ID with a photo of you—mustache, glasses—but the name says Franklin Holder. Who is that, Mr. Darling?"

"I think you'd better come with us back to the station," Field said. "There's a whole lot of questions we'd like you to answer."

"But my daughter—?"

"Isn't her nanny here?"

"Yes, but I'll need to speak with her—"

The detectives followed James to the other side of the house, waited while he gave the nanny instructions, and then escorted him to the station.

The cremains were turned over to the county lab.

Darling was escorted to an interrogation room, where both detectives bombarded him with questions.

There was no good cop, bad cop—just bad cop, bad cop.

They pressed James to recount everything—from the moment he walked into the house that night, to the onset of his wife's hypoglycemic coma, to her death less than twenty minutes after he'd left the hospital.

"Look," Detective Field said, "we've got a mountain of evidence against you for your wife's murder, Darling.

We know you used a fake ID to buy arsenic from Davies Chemicals.

And in case you didn't know—arsenic is a heavy metal. Like chromium, lead, or mercury.

It's not affected by cremation heat. The lab now has your wife's cremains."

"Why don't you save us all some trouble and admit what you did?" Detective Holcomb added.

"We'll talk to the state's attorney on your behalf. It'll look a lot better if you come clean before the lab results come in."

James continued to deny any involvement in his wife's death.

But the detectives kept drilling him, and after hours of repeating the same questions, James began to wither.

Then an officer entered the room and handed Detective Field a folder.

Field opened it, scanned the contents, then closed it slowly.

"James Darling, you are under arrest for the murder of your wife, Heather Darling. You have the right to remain silent. Anything you say can and will be used against you in a court of law. You have the right to an attorney. If you cannot afford one, an attorney will be provided for you. Do you understand the rights I've just read to you?"

"Yes."

"With these rights in mind, do you wish to speak with me?"

James said nothing.

Detective Field nodded to a uniformed officer standing outside the interrogation room.

"Book him."

After James was escorted out, Field turned to Holcomb.

"Not only did the lab find arsenic in Heather Darling's cremains—it matched the sample from Davies Chemicals."

James pleaded not guilty and retained one of the city's most prominent defense attorneys.

The lawyer was prepared to mount a strong defense—but after reviewing the discovery, he advised James to consider a plea deal.

The evidence was overwhelming. The prosecution was preparing a capital case: first-degree murder with the death penalty on the table.

Prosecutors had already expressed a willingness to negotiate.

A plea would spare the state the cost of a lengthy, high-profile trial—along with the media circus that would flood the town, hungry for every eight-second sound bite.

It would also spare what remained of Heather's family the trauma of sitting through each painful detail of her death—followed everywhere by cameras.

James and his lawyer met with prosecutors and reached a deal: he would plead guilty to first-degree murder in exchange for life in prison with no chance of parole.

He had avoided the death penalty—but that was all.

James would die in prison, though not in the solitude of death row.

The Walker family moved into the house in Pepper Pike. Dave Walker took over as CEO of Win-Rite Foods, with Devin Lloyd—who had served as interim CEO during Heather's hospitalization—guiding him through the transition. Everette joined the company, working under his father.

Aunt Sophia devoted most of her time to Jewel, while also handling bookkeeping for Win-Rite. She had worked as an accountant in New York. She never took Jewel to visit her father in prison—Jewel was still too young to understand what had happened. And Sophia dreaded the day when she'd have to explain it all.

Allie did take Byron to visit his father in prison—once.

There had been no courtroom drama. The case hadn't drawn national headlines, but it dominated the local news for days.

More than giving Byron a chance to see his father after a long absence, Allie wanted to look James in the eye—to see if there was anything left of the man she had once known.

THE GAMBLER

Mark Christopher was his name—a good Christian name, it seemed—but because of his un-Christian demeanor, or perhaps for other reasons, his friends and enemies alike had called him Mac C from his youth. Capital M-a-c, capital C. Yes, Mac C was the most cantankerous, stubborn, obstinate, and strong-willed person in all of Macon: the biggest small town in the country.

Mac C was a very disagreeable man, known to initiate a fight at the slightest provocation. His big-boned, six-foot-three-inch frame, on which hung two hundred twenty-five pounds of flesh, aided him immensely in winning most of those pugilistic encounters. His chocolate complexion was a strong contrast to his eyes—black as coals, with an angry, piercing quality—that compelled most men to lower their gaze when Mac C fixed them with his challenging stare.

He was a fashionable dresser who wore Stetson hats, alligator shoes, and silk shirts—an appearance financed by his very "good" government job.

Though Mac C was on the next-to-lowest rung of the ladder as government workers go, he thought of himself as an important personality among his coworkers.

If you had the serious misfortune of finding yourself in Mr. Mark Christopher's office one day, he would be sure to remind you how important he was in moving your request through the proper government channels. Then he would proceed to confuse matters so that your case would be delayed weeks, if not months.

However, all things considered—and because Mac C was still a bachelor—he was thought to be an ideal catch for any of the single women in town. It was a position he took advantage of, hopping from one to the next as a bee goes from flower to flower.

Apart from Mac C's unpleasant disposition, there was one other flaw that marred his character. All men are prone to one weakness or another—Mac C's was gambling. Wager he could, and wager he would, on anything from the smallest athletic competitions to the date and hour the latest expectant mother in town would deliver her baby. But because Mac C was never known to exhibit sportsmanlike qualities when he lost a bet, many avoided taking the risk of betting against him—it was analogous to heads he wins, tails you lose.

One day, Mac C met Lucifer along the road, and because they happened to bump into each other in passing, an argument ensued over who had the right of way. It could have ended there—for the Devil was surprisingly agreeable on this particular day—but no, Mac C would not allow that.

"Look, man, you gonna apologize or what?"

Lucifer looked with amusement at this overbloated mortal, who had worked himself into such a state of rage that the veins on the sides of his neck stood out like ropes.

At this point, it is not certain that Mac C had recognized the Devil. Usually, when old Lucifer emerged from his Netherworld, he would employ shapeshifting to disguise himself—but there was always some part of him he could not change. It might be his tail, which he would wrap around his waist and cover with whatever garment he was wearing, or his horns, which he would conceal beneath a top hat. Most people in town could recognize him; on this day, Mac C did not. But the Devil recognized Mac C. In fact, he had had his eye on Mac C for some time, believing that Mac C possessed just the type of nature that could be an asset to him in his kingdom.

"Mr. Mark Christopher, Esquire, I presume," began the Devil. "Well, Mr. Christopher, I have no doubts about your abilities at fisticuffs as a way of determining who had the right of way—although it is worth mentioning that I am a formidable fighter in my own right. However, might I suggest a game of skill and chance to determine who owes an apology? That would be a more gentlemanly arrangement, wouldn't you say?"

"Man, you sure do talk funny. Are you saying you're afraid to fight me?"

"What I'm saying, Mr. Christopher, is why don't we play a game of your choice—a game... say, dice—to prove who is who. If you win, you'll not only go home with an inflated ego but also a sizeable amount of riches to boot."

At the mere mention of dice, Mac C's attitude began to change. A smile spread across his face, because if there was one gambling game he enjoyed above all others, it was shooting dice.

"Mister, when I gamble, I play for keeps. And when I shoot dice, I go all the way," Mac C said, mustering up all the he-manly voice he could.

At the mention of "all the way," Lucifer's ears perked up—for this was what interested him the most. "Then it is agreed, Mr. Christopher.

Why don't you gather your resources and meet me on that side street there in two hours, and we will roll some dice," he said, pointing to an isolated street that led into a cul-de-sac.

"OK, OK, in two hours," replied Mac C, starting off toward home, feeling that he had made a bold challenge.

Little did he know that he was playing right into the Devil's hands—who would soon be trying to get Mac C to gamble for more than just money. Mac C spent the next two hours running between bankers, bookies, confidants, friends, relatives, and loan sharks, but all he could beg or borrow was nine hundred dollars.

Mac C had trouble raising more than that because the news that he was to gamble with the Devil traveled around town much faster than Mac C could with his legs.

Most people saw this as a sure victory for the Devil and wouldn't invest money in such folly. Others resented Mac C—or had suffered through the bureaucracy of his office—and refused to give him any money.

Mac C set out for the game's location, displaying confidence in his walk—with its swagger and slight sideward sway. Lucifer had spread a large piece of thick green felt on the smooth, tarred surface at the end of the street. At the edge of the fabric, nearest to Satan himself, was a neatly stacked pile of eighty thousand dollars. Mac C's eyes lit up at the sight of all that money stacked so high.

"Shall the contest begin?" asked the Devil. "You can start when you like and play for whatever amount you choose. But remember, all bets are final," he warned, with ominous emphasis on the word "final." "I won't roll the dice for obvious reasons. I'll leave your fate entirely in your hands."

"What do you mean, obvious reasons?" Mac C growled.

"Well, you must know that anything I touch could be engulfed in eternal flames—as you may be one day, Mr. Christopher."

"Who told you that?" Mac C countered. Only then did he get a hint as to who his opponent might be.

Lucifer's brow wrinkled, and he stroked his beard thoughtfully. "I think man's nature is a little more complex than you are willing to admit, Mr. Christopher," he said. "But it is of little import now. Everything tells in time... I believe we can start."

Mac C reached for a pair of dice on the felt. He palmed them and dropped to his knees, shook the dice in one closed fist, and tossed them several times onto the felt cloth. Sometimes they rolled gently to a stop; other times, one or both dice went careening and bouncing off the wall—a barricade at the end of the street that now served as the backdrop for this game of chance.

"I'm just testing the board," Mac C said.

Mac C placed all his money near the edge of the felt closest to him—his paltry stack nothing compared to the Devil's. He placed one hundred dollars a bit further in front of his stack, into the betting box, which was a white rectangle drawn on the green felt.

With a wave of his hand, the Devil covered the bet by floating a hundred dollars of his own vast resources toward the betting box—a movement that astonished Mac C and left him staring with his mouth wide open.

Mac C's first roll of the dice produced a three—a two on one die and a one on the other.

"Oh no," he cried.

"Is that craps, Mr. Christopher?" asked the Devil mockingly. "Did you crap out?" He proceeded to withdraw his winnings by the same method he had used to place the money on the felt.

Mac C placed three hundred dollars into the betting box, and Satan immediately covered his wager with three hundred of his own.

The second pass of the dice was snake eyes—one lonely spot on each die staring back at Mac C.

"Carry on, Mr. Christopher. Continue with this flagrant, reckless exercise," said the Devil, and he collected his winnings again.

Mac C did not hesitate to place another three hundred dollars into the betting box, seemingly undisturbed that his first two passes of the dice had produced two of the three instant-losing combinations: two (snake eyes), three, and twelve.

Lucifer "faded" the bet by putting up three hundred of his own. Mac C shook the dice rapidly in his hand; his lips moved, but nothing audible was heard. The dice tumbled forward. One die rolled out lazily, showing a four; the second bounced off the wall, spun dramatically on one corner, and finally settled with the number two.

"Six. Well, finally a point to work for," Mac C said in a low tone.

No sooner had the words left his mouth than he threw a seven—five on one die, two on the other. He had lost again. Mac C's confidence was visibly slipping. Small beads of perspiration began to form on his forehead and upper lip. Lucifer removed his winnings without a word. Mac C was down to only two hundred dollars.

The Devil eyed Mac C quizzically as he reached into his pocket and pulled out a pair of red, transparent dice.

"What are you doing, Mr. Christopher—trying to employ some improper method of recuperating your losses?" he queried.

Mac C shifted his head quickly toward the Devil, staring him directly in the face. Now it was Mac C who had the sinister look about him.

"What are you trying to say? It's you who should be called to account. I don't know what you're doing to these dice, but I'm sure you must be using some kind of force on them"—which was surely an understatement. "But this pair of dice... well, I think they can ward off any foul nonsense you've cooked up."

"Wait a minute, Mr. Christopher," the Devil began. "I don't know what you think of me, or what you've heard about me, but one thing I am not—and that is a cheat, my friend. I..."

"Don't call me your friend, my friend," Mac C retorted quickly, not realizing the blunder he had made.

Mac C offered the dice to Beelzebub for inspection. He simply shook his head and gestured for Mac C to continue.

Mac C feebly placed one hundred of his remaining dollars into the betting box.

"Are you afraid, Mr. Christopher? If you are afraid, you should go to church," the Devil said, smiling broadly. "Why don't you bet the whole two hundred dollars?"

Mac C suppressed his anger. "Are you gonna 'fade' my bet?"

The Devil covered Mac C's bet. The next roll of the dice was nine.

"Would you care to bet the other hundred dollars on that point, Mr. Christopher?"

Before Mac C could reply, his hands—seemingly detached from his body, as if belonging to someone else—rolled a seven: a five and two combination, depriving him of his number nine. The seven made him a loser again.

Mac C's face went blank. Somewhere in the back of his mind, he imagined that he was being chased by a dozen faceless men and women armed with clubs, shovels, and bats. He ran hard. When they got closer, he would summon extra energy and pull away—but the chase never ended. Now he saw himself in the middle of town, jostled back and forth by people he had borrowed money from to stake this adventure. They tore at his clothing. *No... no... they will crucify me,* Mac C thought.

"Well, what's it going to be, Mr. Christopher—shoot dice or daydream?"

"What?" Mac C began. "I... yes, I'm shooting the hundred here."

As Mac C spoke and placed the money in the betting box, he felt a heaviness in his chest.

"You call that a bet? Aren't you the same Mr. Mark Christopher, Esquire—the man who said he goes all the way and plays for keeps, and all that other super-bad boasting?" Lucifer asked. "Why don't you play for your soul, Mr. Christopher? Of course, your confidence must be waning a bit. If not for that, I'm sure you'd love to have your hands on this eighty thousand eight hundred here. It could be yours, you know—just one roll of the dice and..."

"Fade me," Mac C commanded roughly.

The Devil looked at him from the corner of his eye and placed one hundred dollars in the betting box.

Mac C wanted to avoid the thought of gambling with his soul. He rolled the dice out onto the smooth felt surface. The point was eight. Mac C desperately pursued this number—this eight. He tossed the dice quickly and with precision, one roll after another.

Combinations of every possible number were thrown, with the exception of those that made eight and—thank goodness—the losing seven.

Finally, after a long and tiresome stretch, a four-and-four combination was thrown, making Mac C a winner. He let the two hundred dollars remain in the betting box.

Lucifer covered it. He rolled again—and won. He let the four hundred dollars ride, and soon he won again.

After several successful rounds—throwing first-roll sevens and elevens (instant winners) and making such difficult points as four ("little joe") and five ("fever")—coupled with parlaying his winnings, Mac C, in a very short time, found himself in possession of not only his original nine hundred dollars, but seventy-nine thousand of Satan's own money. Mac C wore a big, broad smile.

His relatives, who did not go near the playing area (it's not every man who can look the Devil in the face), had no clue what was happening on that side street—other than the green and pink flames rising over the rooftops.

"Do you think that ole Satan has swallowed him up?" asked Mac C's aunt.

"No, I don't think so. I think the old coot is angry about something," answered her husband.

There were plenty of people who detested Mac C's pompousness and thought he deserved to be swallowed up by the Devil.

Gabriel, Mac C's father (God rest his soul), had always told him that, while gambling, he should quit when he was ahead. But as Mac C eyed the remainder of the Devil's fortune, there was a hint of greed in his eyes.

He did not heed his father's words. It was more than just greed—he wanted to shame the Devil and send him back to the Netherworld with his forked tail between his legs. Mac C placed one thousand dollars

into the betting box.

The Devil, of course, covered the bet.

Mark Christopher's hand leapt out, his wrist flicking with a snap. He was on a winning streak that wouldn't quit. But Mac C missed his first pass with the dice.

Mac C continued to win and lose, but he was doing more losing than winning now.

With confidence falsely bolstered by a few token wins, it wasn't long before Mac C found that his soul would have to reenter the game as a bargaining chip.

When he reached to place more money into the betting box, his hand grasped nothing but green felt. He looked up into Satan's smiling face, then down at the empty space where his money had been. Lucifer leaned over and stared fixedly into Mac C's face.

Mac C stared back at the Devil; however, the Devil was not someone who would cower before his gaze. Deep inside, Mac C was angry at himself for being such a fool to have gotten into this situation.

"Well, Mr. Christopher, I think we've finally gotten down to what we came here for. What I have here is eighty thousand nine hundred dollars. You can have this amount—and more. All you need to wager is your soul.

But think of it—even if you lose, you win. You'll have unlimited wealth and power. You'll be granted anything your heart desires, except one thing, of course: eternal life here on Earth—and after all, who is granted that?

So, when you finally leave this terrestrial plane, you will come and play. That is, your soul will come and play in my very own playground. You must forget those obnoxious, fabricated tales you may have heard about the kingdom of Hell. Has anyone ever come back to tell you how good or bad it is?"

"Think of it," the Devil continued. "Think how many people would sacrifice the welfare of their own families to be awarded this opportunity. Your fondest wishes—your most extravagant dreams—fulfilled at your command. There are those who would betray their parents, sell their children, for a chance such as this."

All this time, Mac C had been looking up into the Devil's face, shaking the dice in his closed fist. Every so often, he brought the hand close to his face and blew on the dice—but his eyes never left the Devil's face.

Satan was completely unprepared for what was about to happen, so caught up was he in trying to persuade Mac C to gamble his soul.

"It's a bet!" Mac C screamed, and threw the dice quickly onto the green.

It was a short roll—the dice tumbled perhaps three times. The number was eleven. It was a natural, the hard way; there was only one combination to arrive at that number. It was an instant winner.

Mathematics was not what concerned old Beelzebub at that moment. He had been outwitted—and that didn't sit well in his craw. Outsmarting the Devil was something no one did—or got away with.

Lucifer had begun to smolder, to say the least. Smoke poured from his ears and nose. His eyes shifted from their usual light green to a penetrating yellow glow. All his front teeth were exposed in a grimace, each resembling a canine tooth—sharp as pointed daggers.

His skin began to take on a reddish hue and emitted a fiery light. He was just short of exploding with wrath and fury when Mac C tore open the front of his shirt and revealed three amulets hanging around his neck.

Satan, whose long tentacles had just begun to reach out for Mac C, cringed and shrank back with a scowl and hissed at him. Mac C began to speak.

"These protective charms I wear are from my Motherland, Africa. They have been passed down from generation to generation in this country—from father to first son. It is the one thing the settlers never stripped from us. As long as I wear them, your evil can do me no harm. You made a big mistake, you wretched goat," Mac C went on.

"You wicked slime who says he doesn't cheat. How many mothers have you cheated of their children? How many wives cheated of their mates? I am a Black man, and as such, I have been steeped in the traditional religion of my people. I gambled on the element of surprise—and I won. I've taken you. You never had a chance to truly study your adversary."

The Devil had trouble containing himself. His rage could be felt in the air throughout Macon. The ground around that little side street began to shake. A rumble shattered the silence and grew steadily in intensity.

Mac C struggled to keep his balance in the howling wind that accompanied it. He threw his winnings into his knapsack and fell to the ground, grasping his talismans in one hand and trying to hold onto what little surface he could with the other.

The ground opened all around him. Only the grip of his toes and one hand kept him from sliding in.

The upheaval slowed. The rumbles subsided. A calm began to prevail. Mac C pulled himself to his feet and looked around.

Lucifer had disappeared.

Mac C emerged from that side street with his winnings and began walking back toward the center of town.

The townsfolk met him and followed behind jubilantly. Some grabbed and lifted their newfound hero onto their shoulders. Even those who had once shown disdain toward Mac C rejoiced with him—because his victory was their victory. All people triumph when evil is defeated.

9 781963 380958